# Granny's Teeth

BRIANÓG BRADY DAWSON

• Pictures by Michael Connor •

THE O'BRIEN PRESS
DUBLIN

First published 1998 by The O'Brien Press Ltd.,
20 Victoria Road, Dublin 6, Ireland
Tel. +353 1 4923333  Fax. +353 1 4922777
e-mail books@obrien.ie
Web http://www.obrien.ie
Reprinted 1999

ISBN: 0-86278-570-7

2  3  4  5  6  7  8  9  10
99  00  01  02  03  04  05  06

British Library Cataloguing-in-publication Data
Dawson, Brianog Brady
Granny's teeth. - (O'Brien pandas)
1. Children's stories
I. Title
823.9'14 [J]

The O'Brien Press receives
assistance from

The Arts Council
An Chomhairle Ealaíon

Typesetting, layout, editing: The O'Brien Press Ltd.
Cover separations: Lithoset Ltd., Dublin
Printing: Cox & Wyman, Ltd.

Can YOU spot the panda
hidden in the story?

Danny was very excited.
Granny was coming to stay.
She always came
to Danny's house
for her birthday.

Mum got Danny's bedroom
ready for her.
Danny hid his dirty football
under his bed.
Then he stood at the window,
waiting.

## 'She's here!'

yelled Danny at last.
He turned around in a rush
and almost flattened
his little sister Susie.

Granny's hugs were too tight.
Her perfume smelled awful.

But Granny said:
'Let's all go to
**Good Time Grub**
tomorrow for my birthday.'

'**Yipee**!' said Danny.
Good Time Grub was his
favourite place to eat.

Later that night,
Granny gave Danny 50p.
'You're such a kind boy to give
me your bedroom,' she said.

Danny pushed Susie
out of his way.
'Can I do anything else
for you, Granny?'
he asked sweetly.

'Get me a glass of water
for my teeth, dear,'
said Granny.

Danny was puzzled.

But he got the glass for Granny.
Then she opened her mouth –
**and took out
all her teeth**.

'Wow!' said Danny.

Granny left her teeth
on the bathroom shelf
and went to bed.

Danny stared and stared at
**Granny's teeth**.
'Hello, Danny,' they
seemed to say,
in a friendly sort of way.

Next morning, Danny was
getting ready for school.
**Granny's teeth**
were still in the glass.

'Hi, chompers!'
said Danny.

Mum and Dad were having
breakfast in the kitchen.
Susie was playing.
Granny was snoring loudly.

Danny closed the
bathroom door.

He dipped his fingers
into the glass.

He lifted out
**Granny's teeth**.
They were wet and slippery.

Danny stuck the teeth
into his mouth.
'**Yuck**,' he said.
Granny's teeth had
a strange taste.

Danny rinsed the teeth
under the tap
and tried them on again.

He made a wicked face
at himself in the mirror.

Then he had
**a wonderful idea**.

I could have fun with
Granny's teeth at school,
he thought.
Granny won't need them
until I get home.

He dried **Granny's teeth**
on the towel.

He threw the towel
on the bathroom floor
and stuffed the teeth
deep into his pocket.

He ran out of the bathroom.
He grabbed his schoolbag.

He ran down the stairs.

'Watch where you're going!'
said Mum.
She was carrying a tray
up to Granny.
Granny's boiled egg rolled off.
It hit poor Susie on the head.

'**Danny**!' shouted Mum.
'I'm off!' said Danny
before she could say
another word.

There were lots of children
in the yard
when Danny got to school.
'Look what I have,'
said Danny to his friends
Mark and Darren.

Mark pushed **Granny's teeth** into his mouth.
He looked very funny.
'Hello, dear!' he said
in a strange voice.

Then Danny put them on.
'Rrrrrooooooaaaaaarrrr!'
he snarled at some smaller boys
who came to watch.

'Me next!' shouted Darren.
Danny threw **Granny's
teeth** to Darren.

Darren stuck
**Granny's teeth**
out over his bottom lip
'Look – it's Funny Bunny!'
said Mark.

All the boys laughed.
Danny was very pleased that
he had **Granny's teeth**
at school.

'Can I have a go, Danny?'
said Conor Daly.
'No,' said Danny.
'You're not my friend,
Conor Daly.'

Just then the school bell rang
and all the children
went into class.

But Danny could not find
Granny's teeth **anywhere**.

'**Where are Granny's
teeth**?' he shouted.
'Who has them?'

'Quiet!' said Teacher.

Danny was very worried.
He had to find
**Granny's teeth**.

Danny saw Conor Daly
and his friend Tim laughing.

'Catch!' whispered Conor.
He threw **Granny's teeth** to Tim.
They landed on the floor.

Teacher looked over.
'What's going on down there?'
she asked. 'Quiet, please.'
Then she turned away.

Tim kicked the teeth back.

Conor crawled under his desk.
He stuck **Granny's teeth**
in his mouth and
made a funny face.
Tim laughed.

But Danny did not laugh.
If Teacher saw **Granny's
teeth**, he'd be in big trouble.

Mark grabbed the teeth
from Conor and
threw them to Danny.

But Danny saw Teacher
heading straight for his desk!

Quick as a flash,
he threw **Granny's
teeth** back.

## Granny's teeth

flew out the window.
They landed in a puddle
in the school yard.
All the boys laughed.

Teacher was cross.
She went to the yard
and got the teeth.
'You are in trouble,
Danny Brown,' she said.
'Two of these teeth are broken.'

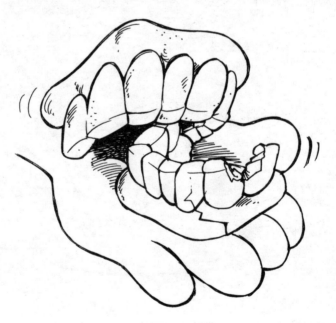

Danny said nothing.
He stuffed the teeth
into his pocket.
Granny will never notice,
he thought.

As he walked home from school
Danny thought about
Good Time Grub.

'I think I'll have
a **giant** hamburger,'
Danny said to himself.
'Maybe Granny will
have one too.'

But Granny was sitting
in the kitchen,
looking very cross.
Her arms were folded
in front of her.
There was a thin line
where her lips should be.

Danny sneaked
up the stairs.
He went into the bathroom.
He dropped **Granny's teeth**
back into the glass.

'So that's what happened
to **Granny's teeth**!'
said a voice behind him.

Mum was at the
bathroom door.
'I have **something to say**
to you, Danny,' she said crossly.

'When are we going to
Good Time Grub?'
said Danny.

Mum lifted
**Granny's teeth**
out of the glass.

'Good Time Grub!'
said Mum.
'You can forget about
Good Time Grub.
Just look at
**Granny's teeth**!
They're broken.
Granny cannot chew
without her teeth!'

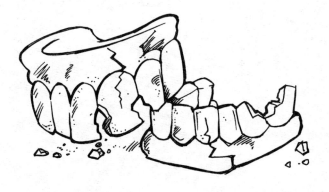

'Granny will have to eat
**mashed potatoes** –
just like Susie,' said Mum.
'And that's what
you'll have too!'

Danny sat at the table
for his dinner.
He looked at the
**mashed potatoes**.
'I hate mashed potatoes,'
he said.

'I'll never do anything
like this again,' he said.
**'Never. Never. Never.'**

*But I think he will, don't you?*
*Danny's just that kind of kid.*

# Books in the **panda** series

### PANDA (1)
## Muckeen the Pig
Fergus Lyons

### PANDA (2)
## No Shoes for Tom!
Una Leavy
Illustrated by Margaret Suggs

### PANDA (3)
## Ribbit, Ribbit!
Anne Marie Herron
Illustrated by Stephen Hall

### PANDA (4)
## Fireman Sinead!
Anna Donovan
Illustrated by Susan Cooper

### PANDA (5)
## Amy's Wonderful Nest
Gordon Snell
Illustrated by Fergus Lyons

## PANDA (6)
### The Little Black Sheep
Elizabeth Shaw

## PANDA (7)
### A Garden for Tom
Una Leavy
Illustrated by Margaret Suggs

## PANDA (8)
### Sinead the Dancer
Anna Donovan
Illustrated by Susan Cooper

## PANDA (9)
### Katie's Caterpillars
Stephanie Dagg
Illustrated by Stephen Hall

## PANDA (10)
### Granny's Teeth
Brianóg Brady Dawson
Illustrated by Michael Connor